LET'S CALL IT . . .
Disney MECH-X4

Adapted by Alexa Young

Based on the series created by Steve Marmel

Based on the episode "Let's Call It MECH-X4!" written by Steve Marmel

Disney PRESS

LOS ANGELES · NEW YORK

Library of Congress Control Number: 2017949651
ISBN 978-1-368-01440-3
FAC-029261-17230

For more Disney Press fun, visit www.disneybooks.com
Visit DisneyXD.com

SUSTAINABLE
FORESTRY
INITIATIVE

Certified Chain of Custody
Promoting Sustainable Forestry

www.sfiprogram.org
SFI-01054

The SFI label applies to the text stock

PART 1

CHAPTER 1

FROM THE FOUNTAIN GURGLING peacefully on the front quad to the students milling around on the concrete steps to the bikes locked up in the metal racks, it may have looked like another typical day at Bay City High. But nothing was typical for Ryan Walker. Not anymore, that is—and not just because it was the first day of his freshman year.

As he pushed through the glass doors of the school's main building and passed by a huge WELCOME BACK, STUDENTS banner, Ryan thought about how crazy his life had become over the last few months of summer break. Who would have ever expected that

anyone—especially painfully average Ryan Walker—would discover he had such an incredible gift?

The truth was Ryan's older brother, Mark, had always been the one with all the talents. Mark was good at pretty much everything—especially sports. Basketball, baseball, football, martial arts . . . you name it, Mark could crush it. Everybody knew he was the most awesome kid in the universe. But nobody knew that better than, well, *Mark.*

That fact was immediately obvious as Ryan caught his brother standing proudly next to a glass case full of sports trophies and ribbons, complete with a framed photo of Mark perched right there in the middle like it was some sort of freaking shrine to him. Actually, Mark wasn't standing so much as he was posing, showing off the bright blue-and-gold varsity letterman jacket that he almost never took off. Ryan had even caught the dude sleeping in it once! He couldn't help rolling his eyes as he watched Mark gaze into the screen of his smartphone and give it a wink while he snapped a selfie and said out loud, "I. Am. Awesome!"

Yikes. It was a miracle Mark had been able to fit his inflated head through the doors of the school that morning! As his brother waved to a group of friends and headed over to talk with them, Ryan kept walking and couldn't help feeling a bit like the invisible man. It would be a serious miracle if anyone at Bay City High ever noticed him. But that was nothing new—by that point, Ryan was used to living in the shadow of his perfect older brother.

Except, Ryan remembered, *Mark isn't the one with* all *the talents. Not anymore!*

Seriously. Ryan had a gift, too. His just happened to be kind of . . . different. At first, he'd thought it was bad luck—like, everything electronic seemed to be out to get him. Case in point: all summer long, Ryan's alarm clock had started buzzing at totally random hours of the night, refusing to turn off until he threw it across the bedroom. Then there was the toaster, which practically attacked him whenever he tried to grab breakfast—literally launching the burned-to-a-crisp bread directly at his head, knocking him to the ground. Of course,

Mark would just stand there eating his cereal and ask, "Are you *sure* we're related?" Even cars threw shade at Ryan. Every time he found himself skateboarding through a parking lot, headlights started flashing one by one, then windshield wipers would start going, and car alarms would blare at him like crazy.

But then something amazing happened. One morning, at 2:00 a.m., he was once again jolted awake by his alarm clock buzzing. However, this time all Ryan had to do was glare at the red numbers on the clock, and the thing went dead. Ryan was about to go back to sleep, but then he bolted back up. Had that really just happened? He stared at the alarm clock again, and with a crackling blue flash in his eyes, he turned it back on. Then, staring at it one more time, he turned it off—just by thinking about what he wanted it to do.

That was it. He had figured it out! Ryan's gift was a special power. He learned that if he concentrated hard enough, he could control technology—with his mind.

Later, Ryan tried to test out this newly discovered talent. When the big Knuckle Crunchers 2 fight was

set to air on TV, and a message on the screen said it would be blocked unless he forked over $49.99, he simply laughed and told the TV to guess again. Then, by focusing hard enough, he made the word BLOCKED disappear and the fight was on! It was too cool.

Ryan couldn't wait to tell his two best friends. But when he found them in the hallway on that first day of school and told them everything that had happened, they seemed skeptical—or, at least, Harris did.

"I don't know, Ryan," Harris said with a shrug. "Those all could have been coincidences. I'm gonna need more proof."

That's when Ryan spotted a vending machine up ahead. "Okay, you want proof? I'll give you proof."

He grabbed Harris and Spyder each by an arm, and after glancing around to make sure nobody else was looking, he stared at the electronic keypad on the vending machine, his eyes beginning to glow. The harder he concentrated, the more the bags of chips and candy began to shake until, suddenly, they were all released from their shelves, tumbling to the bottom and

flying straight out onto the ground. Spyder's eyes grew wide and he laughed hysterically as he dove for the free snacks, grabbing as many as he could. And with that, Ryan had not only satisfied one friend's hunger, but also the other's demand for proof of his incredible talent.

"Reconsidering all the data . . ." Harris lifted his hands in mock worship of Ryan. "Dang, son!"

"You're like a human remote control!" Spyder added, looking up at Ryan, barely able to contain his excitement. "What do we do with this?"

Ryan smiled down at Spyder, who was sitting on the ground surrounded by an abundance of salty and sweet riches. "What do we *do* with this? Anything we want!"

In that moment, Ryan got the overwhelming feeling that high school was going to be pretty awesome after all—even more awesome than it was for his brother, Mark, the super-jock. Best of all, the awesomeness would be thanks to his seriously cool new superpower.

CHAPTER 2

AFTER STUFFING THEIR BACKPACKS

full of snacks from the vending machine and heading down the hall in search of their lockers, Ryan and his friends couldn't stop talking about what had just happened. Although they obviously had plenty of reasons to be stoked about Ryan's new skill, the whole thing was also kind of weird—and, once again, Harris was determined to apply his scientific method to it.

"Did you swim in that lake by the chemical plant?" he asked, clutching the straps of his backpack.

"No." Ryan shook his head and smirked down at his friend, who was wearing a button-down shirt and tie,

even though they were going to a public school—no uniform required.

"Were you struck by lightning?" Harris persisted.

"I think I'd remember that," Ryan laughed.

"Bitten by a spider?" Harris wondered.

"I don't do that anymore!" Spyder insisted. The poor guy had never lived down that one unfortunate incident during their preschool days.

"Then *what*?" Harris demanded.

"I'm sorry, Harris, there's no elaborate origin story," Ryan replied as the sound of a bell echoed through the halls, cutting their conversation short, and then a woman's voice came over the PA system.

"Attention, students, this is Principal Grey, welcoming you to another exciting year at Bay City High." She paused for a moment and then cheered loudly, "Go, Fighting Llamas—and go, Mark Walker!"

Ryan cringed as throngs of students along the banks of blue lockers began pumping their fists in the air and chanting, "Mark! Mark! Mark!"

Then there was Ryan's older brother again,

high-fiving his adoring fans and dancing around to the beat of their cheers as more guys with the same letterman jackets patted him on the back.

"He *is* awesome!" Principal Grey added through the PA.

What the heck? Ryan already knew his brother was popular, but he was starting to wonder if they were in a high school . . . or a Mark Walker Fan Club gathering.

"And to our new students: I know starting high school can be stressful. . . ." The principal's voice became syrupy sweet. "My door is always open—and here's a fair warning: I'm a hugger!"

Finally, Ryan, Harris, and Spyder arrived at their lockers and began fiddling with the combinations as Principal Grey added, "And, older students, go easy on the freshmen. We can't afford another wedgie-based lawsuit. That kid is still walking funny."

Even though there were plenty of students still milling around, the hall suddenly became quiet—a little *too* quiet—and Harris stopped working on his lock and glanced to his left, where Ryan's brother stood leaning

against the wall, staring at Ryan with a huge eager grin on his face. Mark was surrounded by a bunch of his jock friends, who were sporting the same sketchy smiles. Then Mark tapped his best buddy, Dane, on the shoulder and nodded in Ryan's direction.

"H-hey, guys," Harris stuttered, turning nervously to look at Ryan and Spyder, who were pulling their lockers open, "maybe you shouldn't—"

But it was too late. The locker doors exploded open and released a torrent of random papers, along with something gooey and disgusting.

"HURT! LOCKER!" Mark and his buddies yelled, pointing and laughing at Ryan and Spyder, and then high-fiving each other.

"Ugh!" Ryan grimaced as he began to wipe the mess off his face while trying to figure out exactly what had hit him.

Was that . . . ? Ryan shuddered. *No, it couldn't be.*

But, being the work of Mark, Dane, and their friends, that's exactly what it was: a white jockstrap had affixed

itself to Ryan's face with some nasty, gooey brown substance, which had also splattered all over Spyder's face.

"Oh, man, we really stuck it to the newbies this year," laughed Dane, shaking his chin-length brown hair and giving Mark another high five as he looked at the mess they'd made all over Ryan's face. He added, "Good work on those trash flingers."

Mark nodded, patting Dane on the back while actually congratulating himself. "I *am* the king of fling!"

Meanwhile, Ryan finally got the jockstrap off his face—but the thick brown goo remained. "I really hope this is peanut butter in here." Ryan's stomach turned as he handed the undergarment to Spyder, who enthusiastically tasted it.

"Heh, peanut butter *cup*—get it?" Spyder said with a goofy grin as he wiped some of the brown gunk off his face and had another taste.

But Ryan wasn't laughing. "Okay. So, Mark wants to play pranks? I can play pranks."

The wheels were already spinning in Ryan's head. He was going to get back at his brother, big-time. He was going to make him pay. He was going to get his revenge! Just as soon as he got all that nasty goo off his face.

CHAPTER 3

LATER THAT DAY, AS RYAN, HARRIS, and Spyder sat on the bleachers in their PE clothes, Ryan watched Mark run around the far end of the track with some of the other varsity athletes. As the jocks passed by a porta-potty, Ryan looked a bit farther over and noticed a worker getting out of a truck and placing a giant hose into an opening in the ground. *Yes!* Finally, Ryan was going to get his revenge.

"Okay, you guys," Ryan said to Harris and Spyder, "keep your eye on the waste truck and keep your eye on varsity. Let's see how funny they think it is when they're the ones coated in gunk."

But Harris, ever the practical one, frowned as he looked over at the truck. "I don't know, Ryan. There could be unintended consequences."

To Ryan's surprise, Spyder became serious and agreed. "You know what? My friend Harris here, he makes a good point."

Ryan studied Spyder's face, his longish messy hair falling into his eyes. Spyder was usually so chill— always the guy who would go with the flow. "But just hear me out," Spyder continued as his face broke into a wide grin. "Do it!"

Ryan nodded, raising his dark eyebrows at Harris, and smiled. "I'm gonna have to go with Spyder on this one."

Harris shook his head and sighed, but Ryan was already fixing his gaze on the waste truck, his pale eyes starting to glow blue against his light brown complexion. Then, suddenly, something short-circuited and sparks flew everywhere.

"Ah!" Ryan winced as a painful jolt shot through his head. He looked over at the waste management guy,

who was trying to put out the electrical fire that had ignited on the truck.

But Ryan wasn't giving up that easily. He stared hard at the truck and tried again, only to feel another painful jolt as his eyes flashed with an odd crackle. "Ah! Something's wrong with my power!"

As more sparks flew from the truck, most of the students who were out on the field or gathered around the bleachers stopped and turned to see what was going on.

"Turn it down!" Harris shouted at Ryan.

"I'm trying!" Ryan insisted, the light in his eyes flickering on and off as visions of broken-down cars and buses and an old shipyard began flashing through his mind. Then, before he knew what was happening, the giant hose from the waste truck flew across the field and pointed directly at Ryan, Harris, and Spyder.

"Oh, no . . ." the three of them gasped in unison as a stream of nasty, stinking sewage—banana peels, apple cores, and a torrent of sludge—spewed all over their faces and coated their hooded sweatshirts.

Now everyone's attention was on Ryan, Harris, and Spyder. As they tried unsuccessfully to wipe some of the junk from their faces, Mark and his friends and a bunch of cheerleaders all started to point and laugh. But then another girl raced over, waving her smartphone in the air. Her big blue eyes sparkled with determination.

"Hi. Cassie Park," the girl said. "That's CassieP on Gramogram, SparkNet, and EveryVid, streaming live."

Oh, no. She was filming them!

"Now, tell me," Cassie continued, "how does it feel to be the only freshmen ever to be double-dumped on the first day of school?"

"Annoyed," Ryan replied flatly. "Now that it's on the Internet."

Meanwhile, Mark and his buddies were now standing a few feet away, laughing their heads off. "Looks like lunch is on him," Dane said, chuckling.

A hush fell over the crowd as everyone scrunched up their faces at Dane, not getting the joke at all. But then Mark pointed at the rotten food covering Ryan and

his friends and slowly repeated, "Looks like *lunch* . . . is on *him*!"

Of course, because it was Mark, everyone immediately burst into hysterics, like it was the most hilarious thing they had ever heard. Cassie smiled along with them as Ryan's brother leaned into the frame. "Oh, Mark!" she giggled.

As Cassie continued to capture the entire pathetic scene on video, Mark walked over to Ryan and said, "Dude! Now you're gonna be famous for more than just being my little brother."

Then Mark winked and shot two fingers at Cassie's camera before turning to walk away, surrounded by his adoring fans. Completely defeated, Ryan sighed and walked off with Harris and Spyder, who were eager to change out of their sewage-covered gym clothes. Being famous for being Mark's little brother had always kind of stunk—but now it completely reeked. Literally.

CHAPTER 4

EVEN AFTER CHANGING BACK INTO his school clothes, Ryan still felt dirty. How could his power have failed him so badly?

"I don't want to be all, 'I told you so,'" said Harris, smoothing down his straight black hair as they exited the boys' locker room, "so I'm gonna say it in Spanish. *Te lo dije.*"

"Okay, but everything was working fine," Ryan replied with a grimace, thinking back to that moment when the garbage hose turned on him. "It's just I got distracted. It was like a vision. Of . . . abandoned cars."

It was the truth, and yet it sounded like a feeble

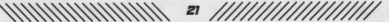

excuse—even to Ryan. But Harris immediately pulled out his backpack to search for something.

Meanwhile, Spyder's eyes glazed over and he murmured, "When I have a vision, it's usually of Ariana Grande . . . and cake."

Ryan squinted, searching his mind for more details of his vision. "Yeah, mine was a junkyard—by a river!"

Harris, who was now holding his tablet computer, began punching everything Ryan was saying into a mapping app. "Cars, river, junkyard," he repeated. "Anything else?"

Ryan thought for a minute, and then remembered what he had seen *in* the river. "Yeah, a ferry—a huge, abandoned ferry."

Harris held up his tablet. "Like this?"

Ryan couldn't believe his eyes—it was an overhead satellite shot of exactly what he had seen in his vision. "Yeah, that!"

The second they got home from school, Ryan, Harris, and Spyder grabbed their bikes and headed out. The closer they got to their destination, the weirder things started to feel. The clouds got darker and seemed to hang lower, the trees were all bare, and there was a damp chill in the air. It was gloomy—even a little scary. But there was no turning back now. They were determined to figure out what was going on with Ryan.

When they got to the top of the hill overlooking the junkyard, a sense of calm washed over Ryan. It was exactly the way it had been in his vision. He nodded over at Harris and Spyder, and they all rode down into the junkyard. After leaning their bikes against one of the rusty old trucks, they took off their helmets and began wandering through the rows of cracked tires, massive pipes, and broken-down auto parts, not quite sure what they were supposed to be looking for. That's when something creaked, rising from a heap of discarded metal, and began to glow. It was shining a giant spotlight directly at Ryan.

"What are you doing to that lamp?" Harris asked.

"I'm not doing anything," Ryan insisted as the white metal arm of the lamp, which was dripping with bright green river slime, bent and extended closer to him and began to buzz, whir, and beep. "I think the lamp is scanning me."

Spyder's mouth dropped open. "If that is a lice test, I am totally gonna fail."

As soon as the lamp stopped buzzing, a series of loud booms echoed out on the river. The boys turned toward the thundering sound, only to see blinding flashes of light shooting out of the top of the ferry. They stood there in awe as the top deck slid open and disappeared and, as the ferry lurched and rumbled, an enormous robot-like figure slowly began to rise from within its remains.

"Are you guys seeing this?" Spyder asked, his voice barely above a whisper as the robot climbed higher and higher until it was towering above them like a skyscraper.

"Whoa," Ryan gasped.

It had to be at least one hundred feet tall—a massive mostly silver structure with bright blue arms, the armor from its shoulders to its hips forming a giant golden X across its torso. At the end of its left arm was a robotic hand, but extending from the right arm was a limb that appeared to be some sort of cannon or missile launcher.

Then, before any of them realized what was happening, the robot raised its right foot above the three boys.

"Aaah!" Ryan, Harris, and Spyder screamed as the giant metal boot cast a dark shadow and came crashing down on them.

CHAPTER 5

RYAN WAS CERTAIN HE SAW HIS life flashing before his eyes—but, as it turned out, it wasn't his life that he saw at all. Instead of getting crushed by the robot's boot, all three boys found themselves inside some sort of elevator, shooting from the robot's foot up to its head at lightning speed as blue lights flashed all around them. Within seconds, the elevator came to a crashing stop and the doors slowly slid open.

"Aaah!" the boys all screamed in unison again as a cloud of smoke shot up from the glowing floor and they were ejected from the elevator.

"Whoa." Ryan sucked in his breath as they took a few tentative steps into a massive darkened chamber.

There were computers and consoles everywhere, columns of blue neon light crawling up the walls, and an orange glow shooting up through the metal grid of the floor. It was like the most futuristic control tower in a fantastic space station, with blinking lights and galactic whirring and beeping sounds all around them. But it also looked like nobody had been in there for years. Unable to resist, Spyder raced over to one of the consoles.

"Don't touch anything!" Harris shouted, slapping Spyder's hand away.

"But I want to touch *everything*!" Spyder replied, ignoring Harris's warning and reaching for one of the buttons.

Ryan dropped his backpack on the floor and made his way toward a pair of curved glowing blue steps that led to a circular platform near a V-shaped window, which appeared to serve as the visor on the robot's head.

Once again, Harris voiced his concern. "Ryan, we don't know if—"

"No." Ryan cut Harris off as he placed a foot on the top step and pressed down, only slightly afraid that something might shoot up at him. "This feels right. Trust me."

Moments later, Ryan arrived at the platform. As soon as he got to the center of it, the floor buzzed and hummed to life, and a glowing white circle with a black X in the middle lit up beneath him.

"Hi there!" A giant face appeared in the visor window, which had now transformed into some sort of video screen, prompting all three boys to scream in terror.

"Welcome to MECH-X4," the guy on the screen continued. He looked like a normal if kind of quirky thirtysomething dude with gray-blue eyes and shaggy brown hair that was partly covered with a black aviator helmet and goggles. "If you're seeing this, it means two things."

Now more fascinated than frightened, Ryan took a few steps toward the screen.

"One: you are a technopath, who can control machines with your mind," the video guy said.

Ryan paused and his heart began to race as he turned back to grin at Harris and Spyder. "Guys, you hear that?" Ryan said before returning his attention to the screen. "I'm a technopath."

"And two: I'm in hiding," video guy continued, his eyes shifting downward as worry flashed across his face. "Or probably dead. Dead would be a bummer."

Harris's jaw dropped and he turned to look at Spyder, but Spyder simply shrugged and said, "Eh."

"MECH-X4 is a complex weapon that can only be piloted by you," the guy on the screen said. "Reach out to it with your power."

Ryan took a deep breath and swallowed hard, then stood tall and tried to channel all his energy. Almost instantly, his eyes began to glow and there was a jolt as everything around him became charged with even more power, including the circular platform where he

stood. Now there wasn't just a circle of light with an X in the center, but white columns of light extended out from that, firing up a larger circle. Then the lights turned from white to blue, and some of them turned off until only the shape of a larger glowing X remained.

"And you're linked," video guy concluded.

Instinctively, Ryan extended his left arm out in front of him, raising his hand and curling his fingers toward his palm. As he did so, the screen became a transparent visor window again, and the robot's giant hand appeared in the window, mirroring Ryan's exact movements.

"Guys," Ryan said, lowering his hand and turning to look at Harris and Spyder, "I'm bonded to this robot. I'm *moving* the robot!"

Ryan stepped forward with one foot, and suddenly the floor shook as the entire robot they were inside of also took a step, the grinding of cranks and gears coming to life after what must have been years of dormancy.

Video guy's face reappeared in place of the window. "MECH-X4 will now mimic your actions."

"So, I bet if I jumped . . ." Ryan paused, narrowing his eyes as he considered the possibilities. As he did so, two blue cables dropped down from either side of him and swiftly placed a harness and belt around Ryan's waist. Meanwhile, several additional cables attached themselves to his forearms, like giant umbilical cords.

Ryan fastened the two sides of the belt buckle, which together formed a blue-and-silver X. Spyder and Harris glanced at each other and held on to the edge of a console, bracing themselves as Ryan proceeded to crouch down into a low lunge, moving one arm behind him and then leaping up as high as he could go. A feeling of weightlessness overtook them all for a few seconds as the robot also launched skyward, and then there was a thundering crash as it landed at the exact same time as Ryan.

"Pretty cool, right?" video guy said with a grin. But his smile faded as he nervously stuttered, "I—I hope it's cool. I assume it's cool. I don't know. This is a recording."

Harris squinted at the screen and shook his head as

the guy continued to speak. "Hopefully, you're a strong enough technopath to operate MECH-X4, because you cannot imagine the horrors coming your way. Monsters as big as the robot, if not bigger. You're gonna need a team if you're gonna save Bay City. Weapons . . ."

There were a few beeping noises as a light hit what must have been the weapons console.

"And defense," video guy added, and what must have been the defense console also lit up. "Now, the most important thing is—" The guy paused, his image on the screen flickering on and off and then back on. "The most important thing—important thing—the most important thing is—".

Suddenly, the screen went black.

"Is what?" Harris shouted, his eyes darting from the screen to Ryan to Spyder in desperation. "That could be important!"

But Spyder was already racing over to the first console that had lit up, where he found a bunch of awesome-looking red and yellow buttons. "I call weapons. *That's* important!"

"He just said *monsters*," Harris snapped, following Spyder over to the console in a panic.

"And maybe he's right," Ryan said, heading up the steps to join Harris and Spyder. "Or maybe he filmed this years ago. No monsters have shown up, so we can do whatever we want with this thing!"

"Don't you wanna know why that guy built a robot specifically for someone with your powers?" Harris demanded.

Ryan shrugged. "Or we can have fun with this thing and do all that stuff later. What do you say?"

Spyder nodded eagerly. "I'm with Ryan."

But Harris wasn't going to let it go. "This is a giant battle bot. We need to understand it."

Ryan scowled at Harris. Why did he have to be so practical all the time?

"When you get a new toy, you read the manual," Harris tried to explain.

"I don't," Spyder interjected.

"And that's why all your Christmas presents only

last until December twenty-sixth," Harris fired back, rolling his eyes.

"Dude, I'm Jewish," Spyder pointed out.

Ryan sighed and looked at Harris, and then walked back down the steps and onto the glowing platform, a genius idea beginning to take shape in his mind. "Okay," he said, relenting, "you're right. Until we can figure this out, we have to be responsible with it."

Harris grinned. "There we go."

"You know, see what it does," Ryan continued. "Test it out. Train."

"Exactly," Harris replied.

"So, we're in agreement," Ryan said, rubbing his hands together and staring at the window.

Harris's eyes darted over to Spyder. "What did I just agree to?"

But there was no stopping Ryan now. He knew exactly where he wanted to go, what kinds of tests he wanted to run, and on whom, and there was only one word to describe how it was going to turn out: *awesome.*

CHAPTER 6

SCHOOL HAD LET OUT SEVERAL hours earlier, but Mark and his buddies were still hanging out in the Bay City High auto shop, making some final repairs on Dane's broken-down classic green Mustang.

"That should do it," Mark said, dropping the car hood so it slammed shut. "Gun it."

Dane sat behind the wheel and revved the engine, making it purr like a kitten. He leaned out the open window, amazed. "How'd you get this beater to start?"

"You give me a set of tools, I can fix anything," Mark replied, wiping grease from his hands before tossing the rag at Dane.

Off in the distance, Spyder emerged from behind a tree and pulled out a trophy. He laughed as he bit the head off the shiny gold athlete like a grenade pin, spit it out, and then sent the rest of the trophy flying toward the auto shop. When the headless trophy landed at Mark's feet with a clatter, Mark bent down to pick it up. He inspected the nameplate on the base, where MARK WALKER, MVP was engraved—except someone had scrawled something else over top of it. Mark squinted as he read aloud: " 'Mark Walker: *least awesome*'?"

Mark glanced around and then shouted into the darkness, "Okay, who's spreading lies?"

That's when MECH-X4 appeared, towering high above the school but too far away for Mark or his friends to see. Inside the robot's control center, Harris turned to look at Ryan.

"And this is responsible how?" Harris asked.

"I'm training, see?" Ryan explained, crouching down on the circular platform and extending an arm. "I'm learning how to pick up Dumpsters. . . ."

From his spot by the tree, Spyder trained his camera phone on Mark and said, "Okay."

"And now," Ryan continued to explain, raising his arm so that MECH-X4's giant robotic hand lifted a garbage bin, "I'm learning how to empty them."

Ryan moved his hands through the air and motioned as though he was emptying a cup, thus releasing the contents of the Dumpster from MECH-X4's grasp. As he did so, Mark and his friends heard a loud rustling coming from the sky and looked up just in time to see mass amounts of garbage raining down on them.

"Aaah!" they screamed, unable to move out of the way before the trash hit, covering their heads and clothes—but mostly *Mark's* head and clothes.

Ryan shook his hands a few more times, making sure to get every last bit of garbage out of the Dumpster as Spyder laughed, capturing the entire thing on video.

"Ha!" Spyder darted away from the tree. "Okay!"

"Now, I'm learning how to take the video Spyder just sent me," Ryan continued, waving his own phone over

at Harris as he tapped on the screen, "and anonymously post it to the Internet. See? Training!"

Harris shook his head and exhaled loudly. "Not what I meant."

"Well, you should have been more specific," Ryan replied with a laugh as he completed the upload. "I cannot wait to see the look on Mark's face!"

Later that night, back at the Walker house, Ryan sat on the couch in the living room, watching the Dumpster video on his laptop. He couldn't decide which part he liked better—the sound of Mark and his friends screaming, or the sight of them completely covered in nasty, slimy garbage. It was a definite toss-up. Hearing a door close behind him, Ryan turned to see his brother walking in—and boy, did he stink.

"Oh, hey, Mark." Ryan casually gestured down at the laptop as he replayed the video clip for at least the hundredth time. "You know, this is only a seven-second

video, but every time I watch it, I find something different to laugh at."

Mark glared at Ryan as he set his things down on the back table. "Not cool, man."

"Oh, but it was when you did it to me?" Ryan asked.

"That was different," Mark insisted with a shrug. "It was a prank. That was funny."

"Nope," Ryan said flatly, turning his attention back to his laptop.

"What, you didn't think it was a little funny?" Mark asked. "Everybody laughed."

Ryan nodded. "Sure, they did. *At* me."

Ryan played the video again, laughing at the sound of his brother's screams. Mark slumped down on the couch next to him, and Ryan shut the laptop.

"So, I'm a—" Mark began with a frown.

"Yup," Ryan interrupted.

"And me laughing at you makes me a—"

"Huge," Ryan cut his brother off again.

"Wow." There was genuine remorse in Mark's voice.

"I know it's always been 'varsity versus freshmen,' but I should have had your back."

Ryan was kind of surprised. Was his brother admitting he was *wrong* about something? As Ryan looked in Mark's eyes, he could sort of see himself in them. They were family, and as different as they were, they were also the same, right down to their smooth complexions and short black hair.

"I mean, you'd never do something like that to me," Mark continued.

"What? No," Ryan agreed. "No, yeah, yeah, yeah. Of course not."

Mark stared down at the ground. "I guess I'm sorry," he said, holding out his hand for a fist bump. "We cool?"

"Yeah. Frosty," Ryan replied softly, bumping Mark's fist back.

But as his brother got up from the couch and headed to the bathroom to clean off the garbage that was still clinging to his hair and clothes, Ryan felt sick

to his stomach—and not because of the way Mark smelled. In that moment, he realized what he'd done wasn't funny at all . . . and it definitely didn't make him awesome.

CHAPTER 7

THE NEXT DAY, RYAN SAT AT ONE
of the concrete picnic tables in front of Bay City High
with Spyder and Harris and watched in shock and
horror as Mark walked onto campus. Instead of high-
fiving him or chanting his name adoringly, *everybody*
now seemed to be pointing and laughing at his older
brother.

"Hey, look, there he is!" a girl shouted at Mark.

"Hey, saw your video," someone else quipped as
Mark shoved his hands into his pockets and quickened
his pace, desperate to get inside the main building
before anyone else took a shot at him.

"Well, you did it, Ryan," Harris said, patting his

friend's shoulder. "You used your giant fighting robot to break your brother's spirit."

Ryan frowned. "Yeah, I—I thought it'd be fun to take Mark down a peg, but now? I feel like a . . ."

"Monster?" Harris looked up, his eyes wide.

"I kind of do. I feel like a—"

But Harris wasn't looking at Ryan. He had turned his attention to something much higher and farther off in the distance, and then he screamed, "No, *actual* monster!"

Harris leapt up from the bench while Spyder and Ryan both turned to see what he was pointing at. It *was* a monster—a giant creature that looked like a cross between a jaguar and a stegosaurus, with glowing yellow spots, spikes down its back and tail, and long, sharp fangs—and it was roaring and bounding on all fours, directly toward Bay City High!

With each step the creature took, the ground shook and students began to scream as they bolted every which way, ditching their bicycles and desperately searching for places to hide.

"What *is* that thing?" Ryan gulped, unable to move as fear froze every muscle in his body.

But Spyder seemed totally unfazed. He held up his camera phone and tried to focus on the creature. "You know, I could probably get a good picture of—"

"Not the time! Not the time!" Harris yelled.

"We need to get to MECH-X4!" Ryan finally leapt into action, grabbing his friends and bolting away.

Meanwhile, the ground continued to rumble and quake as the jaguasaur lumbered toward the high school, where teachers and students continued to scream and run in all directions.

"Single file, everyone!" barked one of the teachers, as if that would help control the chaos.

"Monster!" screamed someone else, running *out* of the school building instead of toward it. "Run! Run! You're all gonna die!"

It was Principal Grey, her face contorted with fear. Then she stopped suddenly on the steps in front of the school and tried to pull herself together, straightening the hem of her navy blazer. "Really could have handled

that better," she said to herself, her eyes darting over to the monster. As soon as she caught a glimpse of it, she turned on the heels of her dark pumps and rushed back inside, while a teacher raced over to an empty Dumpster and climbed in.

Then there was Cassie Park, running toward the thing instead of away from it. "Cassie Park, streaming live on Gramogram, and are you seeing this?" she said in her best reporter voice, holding up her camera phone as the jaguasaur growled and roared, lunging toward her.

By then, Ryan had made it to MECH-X4 with Spyder and Harris.

"Ready?" Ryan called out to his friends, fastening his belt buckle and getting into position on the circular platform, preparing to power up.

"Ready!" Harris and Spyder shouted back, taking their places at the consoles.

"MECH-execute!" Ryan yelled, crossing his forearms in front of him as his eyes started to glow.

Harris shot a sideways glance at Ryan and raised

an eyebrow. "Uh, we're doing catchphrases now . . . ?"

But Ryan was already taking charge, guiding MECH-X4 toward Bay City High, where people were still screaming, "Monster! Run!"

As a group of students raced away from the giant saber-toothed creature, they found themselves running directly into one of MECH-X4's massive robotic feet, which only freaked them out more. "Robot! Run!" they shrieked, turning to head in another direction.

Catching sight of the enormous jaguasaur, Ryan raised his right arm, preparing to activate the MECH-X4 cannon, and yelled over his left shoulder, "Spyder, when I say—"

But Spyder was already pressing the button on the weapons console, prematurely releasing a jet stream of flames so powerful the force even knocked MECH-X4 backwards, causing the missile to go wide and completely miss the monster.

"Whoa!" Ryan shuddered as the creature's rage escalated in response to the missile attack and turned its attention toward MECH-X4. "You fired too soon!"

Spyder waved his hands at Ryan frantically. "Little new at this!"

Harris couldn't resist. "Maybe if you'd practiced a little . . ."

Now the jaguasaur was beyond furious. It pounced across the ground, leaving footprints the size of cars in its wake, and took a flying leap at MECH-X4, grabbing the robot with its prehistoric paws.

"Aaah!" Ryan shouted, stumbling backwards and calling over his right shoulder to Harris, "How do the shields work?"

"Trying to figure it out," Harris replied, clutching the joystick on the defense console and moving it forward as Ryan grappled with the jaguasaur and then took a swing, sending the creature flying back at least a hundred yards.

"Okay, Spyder, let's try this one more time," Ryan yelled, raising his right arm in order to position MECH-X4's cannon.

Spyder took hold of the controller, but he was too

late—the monster was already on MECH-X4 again and sank its teeth right into the robot's cannon arm.

"Aaah!" Ryan screamed out in pain, struggling to keep his arm lifted and finally swinging it enough to toss the jaguasaur aside as sparks flew from MECH-X4's limb. Ryan clutched at his shoulder, wincing. "Why did that hurt?"

"Probably your technopathy," Harris said, adjusting his headset and staring down at the console before looking over at Ryan. "You *are* bonded to this robot. If the robot gets hurt, you get hurt."

Spyder began running a hand along the smooth metal part of his console, petting it like a puppy, and peered up at Ryan from beneath the black rim of his trucker hat. "This doing anything? Feeling any better?"

"No," Ryan snapped and crouched down on the platform, his arm really beginning to throb now. "Harris, you were right. We should have trained. How do we beat this thing?"

Harris grimaced and threw his hands up, but then

he began to work each and every switch and knob on the defense console. "Start pressing buttons and learn as we go!"

Ryan slowly got back to his feet and held up his arms as the monster took a flying leap toward MECH-X4. Harris screamed out and, in a confused panic, reached for a huge black button. When he pressed down, a glowing X-shaped force field materialized, blocking the monster's approach and sending it soaring backwards.

"Bam! Shields!" Harris cheered.

His energy renewed, Ryan pounded a fist on the floor and jumped to the front of the platform, then turned around and said, "Spyder, find me the biggest weapon this thing has."

Spyder turned to the touchscreen above his console, where there was a simulated image of the robot, and began searching through the options. "Uh, shoulder missiles, lasers, and something called a plasma punch—looks like a boss-level weapon."

"But it comes out of the cannon arm. . . ." Harris groaned.

"And the arm's busted," Ryan added, clutching at his right shoulder. "I can feel it."

Then the screen on Harris's console started to beep and he looked down at it. There were four hexagonal shapes joined together, each with a symbol inside— one had a missile, one looked like the circular platform that Ryan stood on, another was a shield with an X on it, and the fourth was a wrench. The wrench was the one that was beeping, and then it moved to the front of the screen.

"A fourth team member?" Harris marveled as it dawned on him. "That's what the four in MECH-X4 is!"

Ryan and Spyder turned to look at Harris, not quite following. Harris looked down at the screen again. Now an image of the robot's shoulder was flashing bright red and the wrench was moving across the screen toward it.

"The fourth person is a mechanic," Harris said in realization. "Someone who can fix the robot!"

As sparks flew from a wall in the back of the control center, Spyder glanced over at Ryan. "I hate to say this, but how 'bout your brother?"

"No," Ryan insisted, still rubbing his injured shoulder. "*Anybody* else."

Harris rolled his eyes and threw his hands up. "Sure. Let's take a break and flip through the yearbook. Maybe the monster will wait."

Staring out the visor window, Ryan suddenly heard something—and then he saw his brother running around the Bay City High parking lot in a panic. "Ryan? Ryan!" Mark shouted.

Without hesitating, Ryan leapt toward the front of the platform again. As he did so, the robot jumped over the roof of the school and landed in the exact spot where Mark was standing.

"Aaah!" Mark screamed as the elevator boot shot him straight up MECH-X4's leg to the head.

Spyder turned to look at the elevator as the doors parted and spat Mark out in a cloud of smoke. "Yeah, we had the same reaction," Spyder said with a shrug.

Mark's eyes darted around as he took in the scene. "We're in a giant robot? *What* is going on?"

Ryan spun around to face his brother while still rubbing his right shoulder. "Short version: fighting a monster, and I think I can beat it, I just need you to fix the cannon arm."

Mark's jaw dropped. "Is there a longer version?"

Meanwhile, a short distance away from the high school, a girl with long black hair was leaning against a picnic table, listening to music with headphones on while punching a text message into her phone. She was completely oblivious to the fact that the saber-toothed monster was now grunting and creeping up behind her.

Noticing the scene, Harris pointed at the jaguasaur and screamed, "It's going to eat that girl!"

"Hit him with the Dumpster!" Spyder suggested, pointing to a bin a short distance away from the picnic table.

"Dumpster?" Mark asked, glaring at Ryan.

But Ryan didn't have time to deal with his brother. He scanned the area, spotted the Dumpster, and reached out with his left hand, guiding MECH-X4 to do the same.

"Hey you, you big dumb cat lizard!" Ryan shouted as he watched the monster getting closer to the girl. "Yeah, I'm talking to you!"

As the girl, oblivious to everything that was happening, continued to punch a text message into her phone—I SAW THIS REALLY CUTE BOY YESTERDAY. YOU SHOULD HAVE SEEN HIM. HE WAS SO HOT—Ryan pulled back his left arm, gathering every bit of strength he had in him, and threw it forward; releasing the Dumpster from the robot's hand. The bin went flying through the air, heading straight for the jaguasaur, and whacked into its head just hard enough to scare it off. As the Dumpster fell back to the ground, the lid dropped open and the teacher who had been hiding inside it stumbled out in a daze and ran off—but the girl, still texting, had no clue what Ryan had just done.

Back inside the MECH-X4 control center, however, Mark knew exactly what Ryan had done—only with a different Dumpster.

"It was you!" Mark fumed, marching over to his

brother. "You dropped all that garbage on me. I'm gonna kill you!"

"Not the time! Not the time!" Harris yelled, his voice getting more frantic with each word as he waved and pointed at the monster, who was now approaching the robot again.

"Oh, no," Ryan and Mark said in unison when they realized what was happening.

But it was too late. The jaguasaur was already in position, taking a powerful spin, and before they knew what had hit them, its massive tail whipped into MECH-X4's torso and sent the robot flying backwards. As MECH-X4 slammed into the ground and slid across a grassy field where two elderly men were sitting at a table, playing a heated block-stacking game, the force of the robot's landing toppled the little wooden tower just as one of the men was placing his winning piece.

"Ha!" the man's opponent cheered, pumping a fist in the air.

Inside the MECH-X4 control center, however,

nobody was cheering. After flying backwards from the force of the jaguasaur's tail, Ryan was in more pain than ever. Lying there on the floor, he lifted his white T-shirt to inspect the damage and discovered a huge dark red welt stretched across his abdomen.

Mark crouched over his brother and clapped a hand to his mouth when he saw what had happened. "Wait, you're really hurt?"

"I can't explain it," Ryan replied, wincing as he looked up at Mark, now beyond desperate for his brother's help, "and I know you want to kill me, but this robot's busted and you can fix anything."

"Ryan, Ryan, calm down," Mark said. "I'll kill you later. What do you need me to do?"

It was time for the Walker brothers to work together. If they were going to beat this monster, they were going to have to set aside their differences. But more than that, they were going to have to recognize each other's skills and talents, and use them. *All* of them.

CHAPTER 8

WITH SPARKS FLYING EVERYWHERE, lights flashing and alarms blaring, Mark ran through a corridor deep in the MECH-X4 nerve center and spotted a tool belt sitting on a metal table. He grabbed the belt and fastened it around his waist as he raced through a maze of tunnels leading toward the damaged limb.

Mark knew he was close to the problem area when he came to a mass of broken piping and wires, crackling and burning so much that the entire area was thick with smoke. Noticing the electrical panels with blinking red and green lights and circuit breakers, he immediately flipped the switches on each box, shutting off the power

so he would be able to make the necessary repairs before it was too late.

Unfortunately, there was no time to spare. The jaguasaur was already back and in attack mode, getting up on its hind legs and lunging at MECH-X4. As the monster repeatedly swatted at the robot with its massive claws, Ryan stumbled backwards on the platform inside the control center. He tried to fight back, but he was powerless.

"Mark, whatever you're doing . . ." Ryan shouted out in desperation.

"I'm still doing!" Mark yelled back after briefly flipping up the clear shield on his welding helmet.

Realizing he couldn't wait for the repairs, Ryan mustered all his strength, squatting down and then leaping forward as he punched the air. As he did so, MECH-X4 launched at the jaguasaur, grabbing it and throwing it back forcefully. Ryan nodded back at Spyder, amazed and impressed with himself.

"Nice!" Ryan smiled as he and Spyder gave each other a thumbs-up.

But taking his focus away from the monster for even a second was a huge mistake. The thing was already back on MECH-X4, whipping its tail across the robot's head.

"Aaah! Ugh!" Ryan yelled, clutching his face as flames shot out of Spyder's console, knocking him off his chair.

"Spyder!" Harris shouted, ripping off his headset and running over to his friend, who was now lying completely still on the ground.

At least Mark was making better progress. "Okay, got it," he noted, plugging in a cable and then flipping the circuits back on. "Woo! Thank you, shop class!" Mark cheered, pumping his fists in the air as the smooth humming sound of moving gears kicked in and MECH-X4's system powered back up.

"Okay." Ryan rubbed at his shoulder and moved it around a bit without any trouble. "Feels better."

Behind him, Spyder also managed to shake off what had just happened, although he was still lying on the ground when Mark got back to the control center.

That's when they heard the angry roar of the monster and saw it bounding at MECH-X4 yet again, seemingly more determined than ever.

"He's coming in for the kill!" Spyder yelled, pointing at the jaguasaur.

"You got this?" Mark asked, turning to look at Ryan.

"We got this," Ryan replied, planting his feet firmly on the platform and bracing himself. "Spyder, plasma punch!"

Spyder leapt up from the ground and slammed his hand down on the red button, activating a simulated cannon arm to the right of his console. Sliding his own arm into the cannon arm replica, Spyder triggered a glowing platinum hand from deep within the MECH-X4 socket.

Seizing the moment, Ryan took a giant flying leap forward while raising his right arm high above his head and then bringing it down, executing a flawless hammer strike. As MECH-X4's glowing hand made contact with the jaguasaur, landing a mighty blow in the center of its chest, the monster shape-shifted and melted

into a mass of oozing yellow lava, then disappeared completely. With the creature defeated at last, the robot's hand retracted into the cannon arm.

"Yes!" Harris cheered, slapping Spyder on the back while Mark and Ryan gave each other a congratulatory high five.

"Um, hey, guys?" Harris suddenly interjected, pointing up at the surveillance screen, where they could see Cassie Park rushing over to the robot.

"Wait!" Cassie shouted, staring up at MECH-X4 adoringly.

"Hi, Cassie!" Spyder shouted back and waved with a goofy grin on his face.

"She can't see you," Harris pointed out, rolling his eyes.

"You saved the school!" Cassie enthused, and Ryan and Mark exchanged proud smiles. "You saved us all. What's your name?"

In response, Ryan's eyes glowed bright blue, transmitting a message to Cassie's phone. Looking down at the large block letters flashing on the screen,

Cassie's voice quivered as she read, "'MECH-X4.'"

As Cassie looked back up in awe, MECH-X4 turned and bounded away, leaving her to wonder when she might see the robot again. One thing was for sure, though: *everyone* would be clamoring to see the footage she'd just streamed on Gramogram, SparkNet, and EveryVid. Her page views were going to go through the roof!

CHAPTER 9

AFTER THE DAY HE'D JUST HAD,

Ryan was eager to sit down and relax for a while with his brother and his best friends—and he knew the perfect place to do it.

"Look at all this," Spyder said when they got out of the elevator and Ryan led them through one of the many corridors and into his favorite room inside MECH-X4—or at least the best one he'd discovered so far. It was like a supremely high-tech clubhouse.

"Man . . ." Mark marveled, looking around at all the gadgets covering the walls.

"Dang, y'all," Harris chimed in, equally awed by their space-age surroundings.

"Whoa, there's a place to chill in this robot?" Spyder said, making his way through a yellow tunnel and then leaping over the back of a half-hexagonal leather couch in the middle of the room.

"Yeah, it's a hundred and fifty feet tall, dude," Ryan replied as the lights switched on overhead, revealing even more consoles and monitors. "It's a lot to explore."

"I can't wait to trick this place out!" Harris said, leaping onto the couch to join Spyder.

But Mark had his concerns. "Everything in there looks really dangerous." He pointed to a room full of strange-looking equipment.

"Everything explody is mine," Spyder declared, waving his arms around excitedly.

"Harris, this lab is gonna be awesome for you," Ryan said, pointing to the area where Mark had just been.

"Check it." Spyder pressed a button on a remote control he'd found, and a huge flat-screen TV dropped down from the ceiling. On the screen was Cassie's website—and then there was Cassie, filing a report.

"CassieP here on the giant robot beat from Bay City High," she said. "CassTag: grateful. CassTag: MECH-X4. CassTag: call me!"

Spyder immediately pulled his phone from the pocket of his puffy gray vest and started punching in numbers.

"Do not call her!" Harris scolded Spyder while pushing a button on the remote to shut down Cassie's broadcast.

Spyder narrowed his eyes at Harris and glanced down at his phone again. "So . . . text her?"

"No. Ugh." Harris grabbed Spyder's phone away as the flat-screen TV disappeared back into the ceiling.

As they continued to explore the different rooms and corridors, Ryan stopped and turned to look at his brother. "Can you believe this?" he asked. "We beat an actual monster today. A giant monster. This is . . ."

"Insane?" Mark smirked.

"Yeah, that's one way to put it." Ryan narrowed his eyes at his brother. Why wasn't Mark excited about all this?

"Over the summer, you learned you had a—a superpower?" Mark was clearly still trying to process the whole thing, no matter how psyched Ryan was.

"And found a giant robot," Ryan noted.

Mark inhaled deeply and looked around the room at all the crazy equipment, a combination of concern and, finally, something more optimistic flashing across his face.

Ryan could understand why his brother might be worried, but he also knew they couldn't let fear get in the way of what needed to be done. "Look, I don't know what we're up against. But I know somebody built this robot for me, for someone with my power."

Mark studied his younger brother's face and started to relax a little.

"Harris, Spyder, they volunteered," Ryan continued, "but I never asked you."

"Well, are you now?"

"Instead of stepping on you with a giant robot boot and sucking you into it?" Ryan laughed. "Yeah!"

"Well," Mark replied with a smile, "we did kick butt out there."

"So, teammates?" Ryan raised his eyebrows and held out his hand.

"Brothers. *And* teammates." Mark grabbed Ryan's hand and shook it. "But do *not* prank me with this thing again."

Ryan laughed. "Don't give me a reason to!"

"So," Harris said as he and Spyder walked over to join Ryan and Mark, "what do you guys want to do next?"

Ryan's eyes grew wide, but he didn't say anything else until he had led them back up to the control center, where he headed straight for the platform. Fastening his belt, he crouched down and shouted, "Let's see what this baby can do!" before leaping into the air.

Finally, Ryan was ready to take Harris's advice and get into some serious training—the kind of training that would help make sure MECH-X4 successfully defeated anything and everything that might try to cross its path

again. The kind of training that would guarantee he *and* his teammates were never caught off guard, and that the whole town of Bay City was safe for good.

Back at Bay City High, Principal Grey was pacing around her office, realizing she needed to get started with some serious training herself.

"Okay, so . . . we need to start coming up with monster drills," she said to the teacher who was standing there with her. "If another one of these things attacks, we need our students to be safe."

The teacher nodded dutifully and grabbed some papers from the principal's desk before heading out of the office to get to work.

As soon as the teacher was gone, Principal Grey tightened her blond ponytail and went over to the window, snapping the blinds closed.

"So . . . the city has a robot defender," she muttered to herself as she sat down at her desk, her eyes narrowing. "Didn't expect that."

When the principal placed her hands on her desk, the surface transformed into a glowing red screen with a variety of creatures flashing on either side, including a scorpion, a spider, a hornet, a worm . . . and, of course, a stegosaurus and a jaguar. She stared at the options, an evil smile playing across her red lips.

"Well, the next monster I make will tear that robot apart!"

PART 2

CHAPTER 1

HE HADN'T EVEN COMPLETED THE first week of his freshman year at Bay City High, but Ryan was already moving through the halls like he owned the place. There was no doubt about it. He had officially arrived—and on his skateboard, no less.

"Hey, guys." Ryan rolled up between Harris and Spyder and flipped the skateboard into his hand before tucking it under his arm, then added in a hushed voice, "Okay, I can't believe we saved this place from total destruction, and we can't tell anybody!"

"Right?" Harris agreed as Ryan took off his helmet and they all began walking down the hall together. "I

wanted to meet Neil deGrasse Tyson! And Selena Gomez. Not in that order."

Spyder looked confused, which wasn't all that unusual. "Uh, were we supposed to keep the whole MECH-X4 thing a secret?"

Harris and Ryan both glared at him.

"Spyder, what did you do?" Harris demanded.

But Spyder didn't have time to respond. Cassie was already ambushing them, waving her camera phone as she took a video selfie. "Cassie Park here with the brave crew of MECH-X4—Ryan Walker, Harris Harris Jr., and, eh, some other kid."

Spyder practically jumped in the air, beyond excited as he grabbed Ryan's arm. "She sort of knows who I am!"

"No," was all Ryan could say to Spyder before grabbing both friends and bolting away from Cassie.

"How does it feel to be the hero of Bay City?" Cassie shouted after them.

Hero? Ryan had to admit it had a nice ring to it— and apparently Cassie wasn't the only one at school

who had decided that's what he was. The moment he rounded the corner with Harris and Spyder on either side of him, he was immediately greeted by what appeared to be the entire student body, holding up signs that read RYAN ROCKS; RYAN IS THE BEST!; THANK YOU, RYAN; and MARK WHO? as they chanted Ryan's name.

Before he had a chance to even let all *that* sink in, a couple of guys were grabbing Ryan and hoisting him onto their shoulders, marching him down the hall while kids continued to shout, "Ryan! Ryan! Ryan!"

Even Mark was standing there, pumping his fist in the air and chanting right along with the rest of them, reaching out to give Ryan a high five—and then there was Principal Grey, welcoming and congratulating him and showering him with praise.

"For saving our lives, for being a hero," the principal said proudly as she stood behind a podium in the center of the quad, "here's a street performer doing the robot!"

Huh? Seriously? As weird as it was, Ryan couldn't help laughing as a guy who was painted silver literally

from head to toe started whistling and busting out robotic dance moves.

"I get it!" Ryan laughed. "*He's* a robot, I *have* a robot."

But that wasn't all. Now a varsity cheerleader was handing Ryan a plate of food.

"A veggie burger that actually tastes good," the principal explained.

"That's impossible!" Ryan laughed.

"And a check for one million dollars! Woo!" Principal Grey concluded as two more cheerleaders walked up with one of those giant checks people get when they win the lottery.

No. Way. Ryan stared at the check. It was definitely made out to him—and it definitely said one million dollars!

"That's awesome!" Ryan shouted over the crowds of students who were now chanting his name again.

He looked over at Mark, Harris, and Spyder, who were joining in with everyone else, pumping their fists in the air and shouting, "Ryan! Ryan! Ryan!"

But then Ryan got the sinking feeling that something was off. The shouting gradually began to fade away, and then it was just one voice saying his name, less enthusiastically and more impatiently.

"Ryan! Ryan! *Ryan*, wake up!"

Slowly, Ryan opened his eyes to discover his mom standing over him. "What?" he murmured. "It was just a dream?"

"Does it end with you being late for school? 'Cause that's where it gets real, kiddo," his mom replied, raising an eyebrow. "Come on. Let's go, Ry-Guy."

Ryan sighed as he watched his mom spin around and walk out of his room. He flopped back into bed. But wait . . . maybe it hadn't been a dream so much as a premonition! Ryan smiled to himself, almost certain he could still hear the kids at Bay City High chanting his name.

When Ryan got down to the kitchen, Mark was already sitting at the counter. Their mom handed them each a

waffle, which was cut up and staked on a skewer along with almost every other possible breakfast food—a strawberry, some kiwi, a rolled-up omelet, a sausage link, and a tater tot.

"Here you go, boys," she said.

Ryan laughed. "Uh, breakfast on a stick?"

"No," she replied. "The Break-Fa-Kabob. It's a new breakfast food I'm selling on my food truck. Try it."

Ryan shook his head but took a bite of the tater tot, and Mark did the same.

"This is good," Mark said with a smile, holding up the kabob in one hand and his smartphone in the other. "Plus, one hand free for texting at the table."

"No texting at the table," their mom snapped, shaking her long dark curls and waving a threatening finger at Mark's phone. "Down."

"No texting at the table," Mark repeated, shrugging and sticking his phone back in his pocket. "Got it."

As their mom headed for the door, Ryan turned to look at Mark, but then something on the television screen over the fireplace caught his attention.

"Wait. Dude. Check the TV!"

The *Channel 7 News* "Voice of Godfrey" segment was on—and next to Godfrey Chamberlin, the reporter, was a picture of MECH-X4 with a caption crediting the image to Cassie Park. But what was Godfrey saying? There was a banner at the bottom of the screen that read ROBOTIC RAMPAGE! but the TV was on mute. With a glowing blue flash in his eyes, Ryan used his technopathy to turn up the volume.

"MECH-X4 almost destroys a school, risking the lives of all inside," said Godfrey. "Now, half of you think that robot is a hero, but the other half . . ."

The news report switched over to a guy in a black helmet identified as a concerned bike messenger, who said, "Imagine for a second a robot foot comes flying out of the sky. You think drivers are bad? Oh, watch out."

Then the report switched to an interview with a man in a hard hat identified as an angry father, who stared into the camera and screamed, "It stepped on my baby!"

What? Ryan looked over at Mark, who was equally stunned by the accusation. MECH-X4 hadn't hurt anyone—and definitely not a baby!

"At least, that's what I'm afraid could happen," the man in the hard hat added.

Ryan sighed, continuing to watch as an interview with Principal Grey came on next.

"It was pretty scary," she said. "Those are my kids, you know? Parents trust me with them. I'm just glad no one was hurt."

Ryan shook his head, shooting a questioning look at Mark as the report shifted back to Godfrey at the news desk.

"Until we get answers, I don't want to say that Bay City needs to live in fear," Godfrey said, his voice growing increasingly panicked as the camera zoomed in closer, "but Bay City needs to live in fear!"

Mark started to laugh as Ryan turned around and looked at his brother.

"What is he *talking* about?" Ryan demanded. "I saved the school. I saved everybody!"

Swallowing a bite of waffle, Mark interjected, "Well, *I* fixed the robot so you could beat the monster, so technically that means *I* saved everyone."

Ryan rolled his eyes and gestured angrily at the TV. "No. This is not cool. We need to get out there and make sure that people know MECH-X is a hero."

Mark nodded. "Yeah."

Unfortunately, they were already late for school. But the moment their final class let out for the day, Ryan would be heading straight over to the shipyard with the others. Then they would find a way to repair the robot's reputation and get the credit they deserved.

CHAPTER 2

SITTING AT THE DEFENSE CONSOLE inside MECH-X4, Harris stared down at his tablet, beyond frustrated. For the past hour, he had been replaying the last few seconds of the video message from the guy who built the robot while running a face recognition program.

"The most important thing—the most important thing—the most important thing," video guy said, static breaking up the image.

Harris sighed and shook his head. "Still no matches on the face recognition app. How is this possible? Who *is* this guy?" He stood up and began pacing. "What

else did he want to say? I mean, it could be anything—like, 'Press the red button and the robot explodes.'"

Spyder's eyes grew wide and he glanced at the weapons console, instinctively pressing the red button in front of him. The moment he touched it, there was a bunch of beeping noises.

"What . . ." Panic flashed across Harris's face.

"Nah, it's a seat warmer," Spyder said, leaning back in his chair, his eyes half closing as he imagined lying on a sunny, tropical beach somewhere. "Oh, yeah, that's nice."

A few moments later, Mark came in through the metal plate in the floor. "Sorry I'm late. I was doing cooler Mark Walker stuff," he explained. Then, "We doing this?"

Now that the whole team was there, Ryan marched over from the back of the control center, where he had been studying a map of the high-crime areas of the city on one of the wall-mounted monitors. "Harris, the video can wait."

"Really?" Harris stared at Ryan in disbelief. "This

guy built a robot specifically for a technopath. Why?"

"To protect Bay City," Ryan replied. "And how are we gonna do that if people think we're the threat? We need people to like us."

"We should teach the robot how to wink," Spyder proposed. "People love it when I wink." To illustrate his point, Spyder squeezed one eye shut while making a clicking sound with his mouth and shooting a finger at the other guys.

"No," Harris said, cringing.

"Uh-uh," Ryan agreed, shaking his head.

"That was the scariest thing I've ever seen," Mark added.

"Uh-uh," Ryan repeated.

"Don't do that again," Harris concluded before turning away from Spyder and giving Ryan a dubious look. "Ryan, this is me you're talking to. When you say 'us,' you mean 'you,' right?"

"No. No, I *mean* MECH-X4," Ryan insisted, heading for the platform. "Harris, are you really okay with people being afraid of us?"

Harris sighed. "Fine. But only while facial recog' is running. As soon as it gets a match . . ."

"Let's goooo!" Spyder interrupted.

"Yeah, let's do this," Ryan agreed, his eyes beginning to glow. "Let's be heroes."

It didn't take long for the perfect opportunity to present itself: an elderly woman was walking along the street when a thug in a black knit cap and motorcycle jacket ran up and grabbed at her bag.

"Give me the purse, old lady!" the dude yelled, tugging at the strap.

"What are you doing?" the woman screamed, terrified, trying to fight back.

"Give me the purse!" he shouted again, finally pulling the bag free and taking off down the street.

"Let go of my purse, you rude young man!" the woman shrieked, and began to chase after the guy.

But the thief didn't get very far before Ryan stuck MECH-X4's giant index finger down in front of him,

blocking his path and knocking him to the ground. As the guy fell, he stared up in the sky at the giant robot, who was now straightening up and wagging his finger at the guy.

"Ah, ah, ah," Ryan said from the platform inside the control center as he wagged his own finger in the air and smiled.

Completely freaked out by what he saw, the thief stumbled backwards, away from MECH-X4, and gingerly returned the handbag to the old woman's shoulder before bolting off. Ryan smiled when he saw the woman staring up at the robot, wide-eyed and grateful.

En route to their next destination, MECH-X4 passed by a park where a little boy was playing Frisbee. As he tossed the disc up into the air, it flew too high and got stuck in a tree. The little boy sighed, intensely bummed out. There was no way he was going to be able to get his toy down from way up there!

Except Ryan had watched the whole thing go down, and he steered MECH-X4 over to grab hold of the tree.

As the robot shook the branches, kids from all over the park raced over to watch and the little boy looked up, amazed, as his Frisbee finally fell to the ground in front of him.

Alas, as MECH-X4 nodded at the kid, who was giggling with gratitude, a woman screamed, "Run!" and the rest of the kids screeched and ran off in fear.

Undeterred, Ryan insisted on continuing the robot's redemption tour—and he knew just the place to go next. He headed across town to Harper Futuristics, the city's most innovative tech company.

"Ah, there it is," the owner of the company, a youngish bearded man in a gray T-shirt and black blazer, said with a smile as he saw a drone flying across the office with a cup on a small tray suspended beneath it.

"Here's your coffee, Mr. Harper," said the drone in a clipped voice.

"Mmm. Delicious," Seth Harper responded after taking a sip from the cup and heading out into the hall, where his assistant joined him with a touchscreen tablet. "Jessica, what have we got?"

"Mr. Harper, if you could thumbprint sign here," said the assistant, walking alongside him.

"Boing," Seth replied, pressing his thumb on the electronic pad.

"And here."

"Yup."

"And here."

"Running out of thumbs, Jessica," Seth interjected with a good-natured smile, finally stopping and turning to look his assistant in the eye. "Hold up. What did I just buy?"

"A company that recycles hot dog water," his assistant said.

"Mm. Well . . . people like hot dogs, they need water," Seth reasoned, nodding. "It'll catch on."

Just then, the sound of a man wailing echoed through the building, and Seth and his assistant spun around and gasped as they saw Marty—the employee responsible for washing the building's hundreds of windows—slipping and plummeting from a towering scaffold. However, inside the MECH-X4 control center,

Ryan was already extending his arm and opening his hand, prompting the robot to catch the worker before he hit the ground.

"Put him down easy," Harris cautioned Ryan as he watched from the defense console.

"I know. Hold on." Ryan crouched down and slowly lowered his hand until, with a small thump, MECH-X4 placed the window washer safely on solid ground.

Observing what had just happened, a crowd began to form in front of the Harper Futuristics building.

"Wow!" a woman said, looking up at the robot.

"Oh, my gosh!" said another.

"That was incredible!"

"Did you see?"

Meanwhile, inside the building, Seth and his assistant were also watching the entire thing with mouths agape.

"Jessica, did that robot just save Marty?" Seth finally asked.

"Yes—and now it's doing some sort of victory dance," Jessica replied, unable to stifle a laugh as she observed MECH-X4 in action.

Ryan couldn't help himself—inside the control center, on the platform, he was busting out a full-on cabbage patch, throwing out his arms and rotating them along with his hips. "I did it, I did it," Ryan sang happily, on the verge of twerking.

"Look at him go!" Seth instinctively began to dance along, with his own robotic moves, as he turned to Jessica and added, "People shouldn't be afraid of this. You—you know that Godfrey person who keeps saying that the robot is evil?"

Jessica looked at Seth and nodded.

"Tell him I have an announcement to make." Seth shifted his attention back to MECH-X4 and gave the robot a thumbs-up, which MECH-X4 promptly returned. "He's doing it!" Seth laughed, thrilled at the robot's response, and raised his thumb even higher.

From inside the control center, Ryan finally dropped his hand and turned around. "You see that, Harris? Your hero, Seth Harper, is giving *us* the thumbs-up."

"I know! I just want to grab that thumb and shake that hand," Harris said with a giddy grin. But then he

quickly shook off the starstruck moment and snapped at Ryan, "No! Stop that! You're doing that thing where you suck me into your crazy plans because they're fun."

Spyder threw his hands up. "It *was* fun!"

"But irresponsible," Harris responded.

"Which is *why* it was *fun*," Spyder pointed out.

"No," Harris insisted, grabbing his tablet from the defense console and focusing on it intently. "I need to get back to that video and unlock its secrets."

"Sure," Ryan said, "as soon as we hit the X deck, turn on the TV, and soak in some of that hometown love."

Ryan closed his eyes and shivered at the thought of it. He couldn't wait to see what the news channels would be saying about MECH-X4 now that so many people had observed the heroic robot in action. At last, Ryan was going to get the credit he deserved.

CHAPTER 3

SETTLING INTO THE COUCH IN THE middle of the MECH-X4 clubhouse, Ryan pressed a button on the remote and the flat-screen TV slowly descended from the ceiling. He immediately turned to *Channel 7 News*, where "Voice of Godfrey" was already in mid-broadcast. Just as Ryan had anticipated, Godfrey was talking about MECH-X4 again. But beyond that, his expectations were far from met.

On a monitor next to Godfrey was an image of MECH-X4 and a caption that read POLL: 80 PERCENT FEAR ROBOT. Meanwhile, on the banner underneath the newsman were the words MECHANICAL MENACE.

"Fear," Godfrey intoned, widening his eyes as he

looked straight into the camera, "is what Bay City should be feeling right now."

Ryan scrunched up his face, confounded. "They're more scared than ever!"

"More scared than ever," Godfrey echoed. "And yet, Bay City's favorite son, Seth Harper from Harper Futuristics, has his usual delusional take on it."

The image of MECH-X4 next to Godfrey was replaced with a shot of Seth Harper, and then footage of him started to roll. "I saw you, MECH-X4," Seth said. "I saw you save Marty."

Spyder tilted his head and looked over at Harris. "Did we save a Marty?"

"I dunno," Harris grunted with a shrug of his shoulders.

"You fascinate me!" Seth continued. "And like everyone else in Bay City, I just want to know more about you. So, mm, five-ish, I'm inviting you to my estate to learn. But mostly, I want to say thank you."

Finally! Ryan smiled up at the screen. "And I will say, 'You're welcome.'"

Harris squinted at Ryan. "What are you talking about?"

"We're going to let him know that we're the heroes inside MECH-X4," Ryan replied.

While all this was going on, Principal Grey was watching the same broadcast in her office at Bay City High and making plans of her own.

"Now that I know where that robot will be, I can destroy MECH-X4"—she whispered through gritted teeth, turning to activate the touchscreen on her desk and then moving her hands across the glowing surface, fusing two images (one of an enormous worm, the other of a giant squid)—"in front of its biggest fan."

Her exaggerated pout slowly curled up into a wide, evil smile.

Back in the MECH-X4 clubhouse, Harris was getting seriously impatient with Ryan. "Are you kidding me?

You want to reveal our secret identities? For *what*? So you can become famous?"

"Trust me, it's pretty awesome," Mark noted, having spent years enjoying all the perks and praise that came with being the most popular guy at Bay City High.

"No," Ryan fired back at Harris, hurt and upset that his friend was so quick to judge his motives. "People are scared of MECH-X4. They think it could be an alien . . . or evil."

"Or an unstoppable killing machine from the future," Spyder noted—and then, when the others shot a confused look at him, he added, "I've been reading the message boards."

Ryan sighed. "But if they see the human face of MECH-X4, they'll be less scared."

"Yeah, especially if it's *this* face!" Mark flashed one of his most dazzling smiles while pointing at himself.

Ryan rolled his eyes at his brother. "It'll be *all* of our faces."

But Harris wasn't buying any of it. "You're not doing this to make people less scared," he maintained,

stomping away from the group and through one of the corridors leading back to the elevator before spinning around to glare at Ryan. "You want a victory lap. What, not enough trophies at home? You want to make MECH-X4 one."

"Zing!" Spyder said.

"Shoots and scores," Mark quipped.

"Okay, let's take a vote," Ryan proposed, raising his eyebrows at the others. "All in favor of proving we're not evil?"

Ryan held up his hand, and Mark and Spyder followed suit.

"At Harper's estate?" Ryan added in an enticing voice, widening his eyes at Harris—but Harris simply frowned and kept his arms firmly at his sides.

"I'm not some vending machine you can technopathically push around," he snapped.

"Weirdly stated, but okay." Ryan frowned as he watched Harris get into the elevator. Was he seriously bailing on them? Did he really think Ryan was *that* selfish?

"If you need me, I'll be trying to figure out why that guy in the video built MECH-X4—because I'll tell you one thing: it's not for fame," Harris concluded, pulling the elevator door closed.

Once Harris took off, Spyder suddenly decided to follow him through the alternate route—the metal plate in the floor of the control center.

So, just like that, the MECH-X4 team was split in two.

CHAPTER 4

"COME ON, HARRIS," SPYDER CALLED after his friend as he chased him down the ramp leading out of MECH-X4's boot and into the old shipyard. "You're not always right."

"If that's the case, why do you always cheat off me?" Harris continued to weave through the piles of discarded junk without looking back.

Spyder shrugged as he followed close behind. "'Cause you're always more right than me?"

Harris shook his head and kept on walking.

"What are you *doing*?" Spyder asked.

Finally, Harris stopped and spun around. "That video was filmed somewhere here," he explained, tapping on

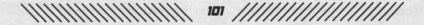

the screen of his tablet and carefully sliding a screen-grab of the guy in the video a bit to the right. "The clues are in this image."

Behind video guy's head were a bunch of pipes and rusted-out vehicles that resembled things in the shipyard. But Harris still wasn't sure of the exact location, or how it would help him get the information he needed. He sighed as he looked up, eyes darting from one area to another, until he spotted something that looked familiar. Yes! That was it! Off in the distance was a dilapidated red Jeep, just like the one behind the guy in the video.

"Hey," Harris said, tapping on Spyder's chest with the back of his hand and then running over to get a closer look at the Jeep.

"Come on, man! You're gonna miss all the fun," Spyder yelled as he chased after Harris again.

"This is important," Harris insisted when he got to the Jeep and began examining it, holding up his tablet to compare it to the image.

"Well, what are we doing here?" Spyder asked.

"Triangulating distances," Harris said, which was met with one of Spyder's standard blank stares. Harris rolled his eyes and added, "It's called algebra."

Spyder chuckled. "Bra. Ha."

Harris glared at Spyder and rolled his eyes. "You can leave."

"Okay!" Spyder immediately took off, yelling "Bye, Harris!" over his shoulder as he ran back to MECH-X4.

Harris turned his attention back to the red Jeep and his tablet. Yes, it was definitely the same—and if that's where the guy had been sitting when he made the video, the camera would have to have been set up . . .

Harris turned around and saw a motor home with a stool and a fuel tank sitting next to the door. It was the only thing in the lot that didn't look quite as broken-down as the other stuff. Harris ran over to it and tried the door. It was open!

When Harris stepped inside, he could hardly contain his excitement. There, inside the motor home, was a bunch of electronic equipment—consoles, monitors, and a whole lot of computers.

"All right, the video file's gotta be on one of these drives," Harris said to himself, heading for an open laptop. He laced his fingers together and stretched out his arms, cracking his knuckles, then slapped his hands down on the desk.

"Harris," he said, leaning over the keyboard and beginning to type, "let's do the work!"

CHAPTER 5

BACK INSIDE THE MECH-X4 CLUBHOUSE, Ryan was standing on the couch doing a different kind of work.

"Hello, Mr. Harper, everyone," he said, his voice high-pitched and shaky, "I'm Ryan Walker, and it—"

Ryan paused and hung his head. "Ugh, it sounds like I'm at a funeral."

He took a deep breath and clenched his fists. "Okay," he said, puffing up his chest and launching into his best attempt at a radio announcer voice, picturing himself on a huge concert stage. "Bay City, are you ready—" But before he could finish, he heard someone

coming up behind him and turned to see Mark. Deflated and a little embarrassed, he turned back around and weakly added in a cracking voice, "To rock?"

"And the crowd goes into a coma!" Mark laughed, pumping his fists in the air.

Ryan scowled and slumped down on the couch.

"Look, I get it, you're excited," Mark said, sitting down next to his brother and adopting a fatherly tone as he draped an arm around Ryan's shoulder. "I mean, I'm used to being the center of attention, but it's new for you."

"Is this your first pep talk?" Ryan narrowed his eyes at Mark. "'Cause you're terrible at it."

But Mark kept on going. "When I was nervous before a game, you know what Dad used to tell me?"

"What?"

"No matter what"—Mark reached out and grabbed Ryan's hand, pulling him up—"stand tall, be confident, and see your victory."

Mark extended an arm in front of him, in a "picture this" gesture, and Ryan stood back up on the couch

and squared his shoulders while his brother continued, "Now, imagine yourself in the palm of that robot. . . ."

"Okay, okay, yeah." Ryan smiled and stood even taller.

"And it lowers us down to the ground; it opens its hand in front of all those people," Mark said, lunging forward a bit and unfurling his own hand as he turned to look back at Ryan. "Cool, right?"

"Very." Ryan nodded and his whole face brightened. "Okay. Then?"

"Then they go, 'Oh, man! Is that Mark Walker? He's so cool! He must be the pilot of MECH-X4!'" Ryan's brother started pumping his fists in the air again and began to dance around behind the couch as he shouted, "Mark! Mark! Mark! Mark! Mark! Mark! Mark!"

To wrap things up, Mark winked at Ryan, dabbing in his direction and concluding, "Good talk, Bro!"

Ryan cringed as he watched his brother take off down the hallway toward the elevator while continuing to chant his own name . . . over and over and over again.

"That was a *terrible* talk," Ryan said with a sigh.

But as poorly as things were going for Ryan, Harris was faring even worse out in the mobile home. Sitting with the laptop perched on a table in front of him, he slumped over and rested his head in his hand, all the adrenaline and excitement fading away.

"Nothing." Harris frowned and held up a disc. "And this was the last one."

Defeated, he hurled the disc across the motor home, where it smacked into a small plastic wall-mounted box. But as the disc made contact, it knocked the lid off the box, revealing a glowing blue square.

"What?" Harris gasped, jumping up and walking over to examine this new discovery. "Oh, man!"

Meanwhile, Spyder was just coming through the floor of the MECH-X4 control center, where Ryan and Mark were also returning.

"Hey, any chance to get Harris to come?" Ryan asked Spyder, but Spyder simply shrugged.

Little did they know Harris was finally making some

progress; after he pressed the glowing blue button, it beeped and a hidden door in the motor home slid open to reveal a secret office. He stepped inside and started to check the place out.

"Whoa." Harris exhaled deeply as he looked around at all the sketches taped to the walls—pictures of what must have been early concepts for MECH-X4—and then a lab coat hanging in one corner with a name tag on it that said LEO.

"Leo?" Harris tilted his head and nodded. "His name was Leo."

Then something else caught his eye—a pile of books, including a black leather-bound notebook with a tag that read MECH-X4 IDEAS on the cover. Harris sucked in his breath as he picked it up and started flipping through the pages, which contained even more early sketches of the robot. But that's when he made the best discovery of all: tucked behind the pile of books was a video camera. *The* video camera? It had to be.

"Yes!" Harris shouted, turning it on. If he could find

more footage on there then maybe, just maybe, he could finally report back to the others with information about "the most important thing" Leo the video guy had been trying to tell them.

CHAPTER 6

EAGER AS RYAN WAS TO GO MEET
with Seth Harper so he could prove once and for all
that MECH-X4 was anything but evil, he couldn't help
hesitating when he looked at the empty chair behind
the defense console where Harris normally sat.

"It just doesn't feel right," Ryan said, frowning. They
were supposed to be a team. How were they going to
prove themselves unless all four of them were there,
together?

"You guys can make up after we're back—let's get
famous!" Mark flashed a huge smile as he looked from
Ryan to Spyder and then back to Ryan. "Well, *you* guys
get famous. I'm already a legend."

Ryan rolled his eyes at his brother but figured he didn't exactly have a choice—not unless Harris miraculously showed up.

"All right." Ryan shook out his arms, trying to get loose and relaxed as he reluctantly made his way over to the platform and snapped on his belt. "Showtime."

Spyder grinned and sat at the weapons console while Ryan threw down the "MECH-execute!" catchphrase. Then, with eyes aglow, Ryan began to run, guiding the robot over to Seth Harper's house, completely oblivious to what Harris was in the process of discovering.

There, in the motor home, Harris had accessed more video footage, and he was watching intently as Leo explained everything.

"The most important thing is the monsters are sent by people—terrible people," Leo said, an urgency in his voice. "That's why I built MECH-X4 . . . so you could stop them, Ryan."

Harris did a double take. "Wait, did he just say Ryan's name?" He pressed the rewind button.

"So you could stop them, Ryan," Leo said again.

"But you have to keep your identity a secret. If they know you're in there, these people will strike directly at you and everyone you know."

"Oh, no," Harris gasped. He leapt to his feet and raced for the trailer door.

But as soon as he got outside, he heard a loud whooshing sound and looked up just in time to see the robot bounding away, its heavy footsteps shaking the ground with each stride.

Panic-stricken, Harris grabbed the phone from his pocket and called Ryan, whose phone started to buzz somewhere on the floor of the control center behind him. Ryan was oblivious to the fact that Harris was trying to reach him—he was too focused on getting to Seth Harper's place.

Harris punched in a quick, desperate text instead: DO NOT REVEAL YOURSELVES! YOU ARE IN DANGER!

Then, searching the area around him, Harris lifted a tarp and discovered a bike and helmet. Sure, the bike was pink and covered in flowers, complete with a matching basket, and the helmet was purple and

designed for the head of an eight-year-old girl, but . . .

"Desperate times," Harris told himself with a sigh.

He put on the helmet, clicking the strap closed beneath his chin, zipped up his blue windbreaker, and rang the little bike bell a few times as he got onto the seat and headed out. He had to stop Ryan and the others from revealing their identities, before it was too late.

CHAPTER 7

STANDING ON THE EXPANSIVE FRONT

patio of his ultramodern home, which, much like his office headquarters, was all angles and clean lines and constructed almost entirely of glass, Seth Harper checked his watch and turned to his assistant.

"I did say five o'clock, right?"

"Yes," Jessica replied.

"Right." Seth shoved his hands into his pockets and looked up at the rain clouds, which were growing darker by the second.

"So, how does it feel to get stood up at your own party?" asked Godfrey, an amused smile on his lips.

"No need to be smug, Godfrey," Seth said. "Could just be fashionably late."

"Ha." Godfrey scoffed.

"Ha." Seth sneered back at the reporter with an irritated shrug.

But indeed, back in the MECH-X4 control center, Ryan was sitting on the floor, exhaling loudly and then turning to look up at his brother. "What are we waiting for?"

"We need to be fashionably late," Mark said with an incredulous laugh. "Is this your first time being invited to a party?"

Spyder crossed his arms and stared at the ground. "Yeah."

At least Harris was catching up to them, though. Speeding along the bike path, he rang the bell a few more times and turned toward the Harper estate. As he got closer to the driveway, he saw a crowd of people and a line of news vans stopped at a barricade near a small wooden security shed. Determined, Harris pumped the bike pedals harder.

"What do you mean 'no entrance'?" Cassie Park was demanding as she shot daggers at the security guard on the other side of the barricade. "I'm Cassie Park. I broke the story on MECH-X4."

"Good for you," the guard muttered, looking past Cassie at the rest of the news crews and waving his arms threateningly as he yelled at them, "Private meeting!"

Ding, ding.

"Well, what about that girl?" Cassie snapped at the guard as Harris sped right past the barricade.

"I'm a boy on a girl's bike!" Harris yelled back at them without slowing down, ringing the bell a few more times. "And that was sexist!"

Meanwhile, Seth Harper was giving up hope.

"Shoot," he groaned. "Well, I guess we may as well wrap this up."

But the moment Seth turned to head inside with Jessica and the other members of his staff, MECH-X4 touched down on the sprawling front lawn of the estate with a thundering crash so powerful that the resulting

gust of wind knocked Seth and everyone near him to the ground.

Stumbling back to his feet, Seth turned around and looked up at the robot.

"Woo-hoo! Magnificent!" Seth cheered, while Jessica and Godfrey simply stared up at the robot, openmouthed. "Look at that technology. I wonder what it is."

"Ratings, that's what!" Godfrey replied, spinning around and barking at his camera crew, "You better get this. Get all of this!"

"You made it! Fantastic!" Seth smiled as he shouted up at the robot, eager to get straight to the meeting. "First off, thank you for coming, MECH-X4. I—I know that some people are afraid of you!"

Pushing ahead of Seth, Godfrey stared up at the robot and shouted into a microphone, "What is your secret agenda?"

Seth shoved Godfrey aside and turned back to address MECH-X4. "But I want to change all that! Maybe if we got to know you more! Where are you from? Are you alive? Are—are you remote-controlled?"

"Are you here to enslave us?" Godfrey interrupted again.

Inside the control center, Mark looked over at Ryan. "Well, what are you waiting for?" he asked, clapping his hands, eyes wide with anticipation. "Fame awaits!"

"Yeah, let's do this!" Ryan punched the air, desperately trying to muster some enthusiasm, but when he caught sight of that empty chair at the defense console again, he sighed. "I just—I wish Harris was here."

Little did he know, Harris had just tossed aside his bike and helmet and was now racing toward the front lawn of the Harper estate.

"Hey! Look at your phone!" Harris shouted up at the robot, waving his arms frantically and then pulling out his phone and pointing at it.

Inside the control center, Spyder saw Harris on the surveillance monitor and called over to Ryan, "I think he is."

Ryan spun around to see what Spyder was talking about. It *was* Harris!

"Look . . . at . . . your . . . phone," Ryan said as he slowly deciphered what Harris was trying to tell him. He reached over and picked up his phone from the ground and read the text message Harris had sent earlier: DO NOT REVEAL YOURSELVES! YOU ARE IN DANGER!

Ryan shook his head and laughed, then went back to the platform, where he could see Harris waving his arms down below. "Dude, this again?" Ryan shouted at him. "Lighten up!"

But just then, the ground began to shake and quake so furiously that Harris stumbled, and even Ryan lost his footing on the MECH-X4 platform up above. As the terrifying tremors intensified, Harris spun around, trying to locate the source of all the thumping and thrashing. That's when a monstrous slithering, slimy green tentacle came into view.

CHAPTER 8

THE MOMENT HE SAW THE MONSTER—
a giant green worm with glowing yellow spots and
crazy squid-like tentacles at both ends—Harris's eyes
doubled in size, his jaw dropped open, and he spun
around and began to run, terror silencing the screams in
his throat. But it was too late—as the massive sqworm
sped toward him with glowing red eyes, ripping up the
ground as it rippled and surged, it uprooted the wooden
security shed and sent it flying straight for him.

High above in the MECH-X4 control center, Ryan
was watching the entire scene unfold along with Spyder
and Mark. Then, like a scene out of *The Wizard of
Oz* gone seriously wrong, the shed landed on top of

Harris, flattening him completely. There weren't even any perfectly shined black dress shoes sticking out from underneath.

"No!" Spyder shouted, while Mark gasped and smacked his hands over his mouth.

"Harris!" Ryan screamed.

After a moment of awestruck silence, Spyder shook his head and stammered, "He's . . . he's . . . dead? No! No, no, no!"

Overcome with grief and guilt, Ryan's eyes glazed over. "He told us not to do this. He told us not to do this and I didn't listen, and now he's . . . he's dead."

Meanwhile, the massive green sqworm was continuing to slither toward the Harper estate, sending Seth, Jessica, and Godfrey into a panic of their own.

"Ryan!" Mark yelled as he raced over to the platform. "We're under attack. We need you. People are in danger!"

But Ryan just stood there in a complete stupor.

"Ryan!" Mark shouted louder.

Ryan blinked a few times, struggling to regain his focus—and, finally, as the giant tentacles snaked around MECH-X4's legs, sending tremors up into the control center and forcing Ryan to stumble backwards, a renewed sense of purpose and rage took over and surged through him.

"This thing killed Harris!" he yelled, preparing for the fight of his life.

"Wait, wait!" Spyder called over, frantically pressing a series of buttons near the weapons console.

"What?" Ryan demanded.

"Zoom in," Mark said, running up behind Spyder to check out the surveillance monitor. Spyder was scanning the area where Harris had been crushed and he was almost certain he could hear someone coughing. Could it be? Yes—it was Harris!

"See? He's still moving!" Spyder pointed at the screen, relief in his voice.

Briefly, Ryan snapped out of his rage. "Well, let's keep him that way," he said before holding up his

arms in a defensive pose, desperately trying to shield MECH-X4 from the tentacles that were still attempting to surround him.

But Spyder could see and hear Harris on the monitor, and based on his friend's screams, he could tell that time was running out.

"Ryan!" Harris yelled. "Ryan, help!"

"He's gonna get crushed down there!" Spyder shouted.

"Okay," Mark said, giving Spyder's shoulder a pat before heading toward the elevator. "I'll get him. Just give me cover."

"You got it," Spyder replied.

"Mark, please!" Ryan called out, and Mark turned around to see the desperation in his brother's eyes. "He's our best friend. And this is my fault."

Mark nodded, accepting the challenge, and got in the elevator. Ryan planted his feet firmly on the platform. Now it wasn't just time for the fight of *his* life—it was time for the fight to save Harris's.

CHAPTER 9

WHILE MECH-X4 TANGLED WITH THE

giant sqworm monstrosity, the scene at the Harper estate was one of chaos and confusion. Seth was the only one who wasn't terrified. Instead, he was viewing the whole thing as if it was a fascinating new development in his research.

"Whoo! That thing is dangerous," Seth marveled, waving his arms as he watched the vicious battle. "Get him!"

But then, a warning bell—or, rather, the *ding-ding* of a bicycle bell—rang out, and Seth's enthusiasm turned to genuine anxiety.

"Down!" Seth screamed at Godfrey and Jessica,

pulling them both with him as he ducked just in time to escape a pink bicycle, which zipped by mere inches from their heads and shattered a window.

"That robot is trying to kill us!" Godfrey screeched.

But Seth shook his head and stole a quick peek. "No, look," he pointed out as MECH-X4 blocked one of the tentacles and shoved it away before it could whip into the house. "It's trying to save us!"

"Sir," Jessica gasped, "we need to get you to safety!"

"And me?" Godfrey asked.

"I suppose," Jessica replied.

"Go!" Seth shouted, darting away with the others just as MECH-X4 ripped one of the tentacles from the sqworm's body, releasing a massive stream of sticky yellow slime.

"Oh! Ugh!" Harris spat after the thick liquid splashed down onto the top of the broken shed and began oozing and dripping through cracked panels of wood, covering his entire head. "It's so . . . so, so gross!"

Although the severed tentacle was a small victory for MECH-X4, Spyder and Ryan were struggling to

push the sqworm back. It was getting dangerously close to crushing the Harper estate *and* the shed—and Mark couldn't possibly leave the safety of the robot and get to Harris with that thing on the loose.

"I'm trying to keep him away, but without Harris, we don't have anyone manning the shields," Spyder called out to Ryan.

"Well, someone has to protect them!" Ryan yelled back as the sqworm slammed into MECH-X4 again, hurling Ryan backwards through the control center. "Aah!"

Harris felt like he might hurl, himself, thanks to all the slime. "This is worse than my mom's cooking!" he groaned, spitting out more of the nasty yellow liquid.

Finally, Ryan found his footing and took a giant leap forward, launching MECH-X4 far enough away from the monster and close enough to the shed that he could plant the robot's boot on the ground. "Go for it, Mark!" he shouted to his brother, who immediately raced down the ramp.

"He's out!" Spyder cheered.

"Harris!" Mark shouted, running over to the shed and peering between the slats. "Harris!"

"Mark!" Harris yelled back as Ryan's brother began to pry a few planks of wood free.

But while Mark grabbed Harris from the shed, the monstrous sqworm was grabbing MECH-X4 and sparks were literally flying inside the control center.

"Ow!" Ryan screamed, clutching at his chest and desperately trying to power through. He could see how close the sqworm was getting to the shed now. He had to do something before it killed Harris *and* his brother! He raised up an arm and went for it, causing MECH-X4 to pummel the thing with a force so intense it went flying . . . and landed directly on top of the shed!

"Aaah!" Harris screamed.

"Whoa!" Mark shouted, pulling Harris away just in time and heading for the safety of MECH-X4.

Staring out at the carnage, Ryan heard a puff of smoke behind him and spun around to see Harris and Mark emerging from the elevator.

"Harris! You're okay!" Ryan bolted across the

platform and cradled his friend's slime-covered face in his hands. He had never been so happy to see anyone in his life.

"Uh, awkward." Harris grimaced.

Mark raised his arms. "I'm fine, too, everybody."

Harris gave Mark's arm a light pat just as a shadow blocked out most of the light in the control center.

"N—not the time!" Harris shouted, pointing at the giant tentacles that had suctioned to the front of MECH-X4's helmet, covering the entire visor window. "Not the time!"

Harris, Spyder, and Mark all rushed over to their stations while Ryan raised his arms, curling his fingers in the air and guiding the robot to grab both ends of the sqworm and throw the monster as far as it possibly could.

"All right! Let's focus!" Ryan shouted, shaking out his arms and glancing over his right shoulder at Harris. "Any advice, dude?"

Harris smiled and calmly replied, "Let's be heroes."

Ryan nodded at Harris and then turned back around,

exhaling hard as the sqworm made another approach. He crossed his forearms in a MECH-execute block that instantly knocked the creature back.

"Let's end this!" Ryan shouted with a smile.

"Have I shown you guys what I call the plasma ax?" Spyder grinned while flipping up a red switch on his console.

"When did you have time to figure out we had a plasma ax?" Harris asked.

Spyder shot an offended look at Harris. "I do stuff," he retorted. Then, slamming his fist on a glowing red button, he activated the simulated cannon arm to the right of his console and slid his arm inside. Harris nodded at him approvingly.

"MECH-execute!" Ryan shouted, crossing his forearms once again and then raising the right one up to perform a karate blow. As he did so, a glowing double-sided ninja ax with two enormous blades spun out from deep within the MECH-X4 cannon arm.

Now totally in sync, Ryan leapt into the air while

Spyder pulled his simulated cannon arm back, readying for the punch, and Harris manned the shields. Then, sweeping his arm through the air, Ryan guided the plasma ax down, splitting the hideous creature in two and releasing another massive stream of yellow slime.

"Yes!" Spyder shouted, pumping his fist in the air.

"Yes!" Harris echoed.

Back in her office at Bay City High, Principal Grey screamed in agony, slamming her hands down on her glowing desktop and sweeping everything off its surface and onto the ground. As she did so, one half of the sqworm she had created—the half that hadn't turned to slime—slithered away and disappeared into a giant crater in the ground.

"Everyone safe?" Ryan asked, looking around the control center.

"Yeah, dude," Mark replied. "How about you?"

"A little beaten up," Ryan admitted. "But if everyone's okay? I'm great."

With that, Ryan lunged down onto the platform and then leapt into the air, launching MECH-X4 and guiding the robot back to the shipyard.

As a gust of wind blew across the back lawn in MECH-X4's wake, Seth Harper stared after the robot and sighed. "How amazing."

CHAPTER 10

AS SUCCESSFUL AS THE BATTLE WITH the giant sqworm had been, the entire MECH-X4 team now knew their work was far from over. Not only had the robot sustained serious damage, but they were in the process of learning about everything Harris had discovered from the video footage he'd found in the motor home.

"Well, fixing this is gonna take a while," Mark noted, studying a damage readout on his tablet and then turning to grab his tool belt and a bunch of wires, cables, and replacement parts.

Harris looked over at Mark and smiled. "Hey, thanks for the save."

"Yeah, man," Mark replied with a nod. "We're teammates."

As Mark headed off to make the repairs, Ryan and Harris leaned back against opposite walls in the clubhouse, and Harris continued to walk Ryan through everything he had learned about Leo, MECH-X4, and the monsters.

"So, um, people are *making* these monsters?" Ryan asked.

Harris nodded. "And that guy in the video knew *you* would be the technopath that piloted MECH-X4—he knew your name."

"Yep, that's creepy," Spyder interjected. "Borderline illegal."

"Huh." Ryan's face clouded over with worry as he and Harris followed Spyder over to the couch.

"Somebody is planning something big," Harris continued. "We have to fight smarter."

"Well, you're the smartest guy I know," Ryan said, beyond grateful to his friend for working so hard to figure all that stuff out. "And you were awesome out there."

As Ryan and Harris continued to discuss possible next steps, Spyder hit the remote control and the flat-screen TV dropped down from the ceiling.

"Hey, guys, they're talking about us," Spyder said, and they all looked over at the screen, where "Voice of Godfrey" was on.

But now, next to the image of the robot, was a caption that read: WHY YOU SHOULD FEAR MECH-X4.

"And a girl's bike goes flying past my head," Godfrey was saying. "I didn't panic. Instead, I saved Seth Harper and his assistant. But that MECH-X4 is dangerous."

"No." Ryan had had enough—and, at last, thanks to Harris, he knew they had more important things to do than change the public's perception of MECH-X4. So, with a flash of blue glowing in his eyes, he turned off the news report. "I don't care what they say. We know who we are—and we need to keep that a secret."

Harris nodded. Finally, they were all on the same page, working together. He didn't have to convince Ryan to listen to him anymore. They all had each other's backs now.

But of course there had been plenty of disappointments along the way, and keeping their identities a secret wasn't necessarily going to be easy, for all sorts of reasons. Acknowledging that fact, Spyder turned to Harris and said, "You know, sorry you didn't get to meet Harper, dude."

"Yeah, or his assistant, Jessica," Harris added, shooting a smile at Ryan and Spyder and waving a finger from one to the other. "I mean, seriously, am I the only one noticing the ladies?"

They all laughed and Ryan held out his fist. "Best friends?"

"Best friends," Harris agreed, bumping his fist into Ryan's.

"Yep," Spyder chimed in, joining his fist with the others, "three equally good friends. Uh, probably impossible to rank us."

"Yup." Harris and Ryan nodded, then got up and walked away. It was time to get back to work—to figure out how to prepare for whatever horrors might be waiting for them on the horizon.

"Right?" Spyder called after them.

But they were already out of earshot.

Later that night, Harris decided to head back to the MECH-X4 lab in hope of making more discoveries that might help the team. But as he worked, he started to get an uncontrollable itch on his right arm. He scratched at it through the sleeve of his blue dress shirt, but that only made it worse.

"Ow!" Harris frowned and rolled up his sleeve to see if there was some sort of rash there. But what he saw was worse than a rash—*way* worse—and his eyes grew wide with terror as he inspected it.

How could this be? Just beneath the surface of his skin, a network of veins appeared to be glowing bright yellow—just like the spots on the sqworm, and on the jaguasaur before it, and just like the slime that had come out of both monsters after MECH-X4 had torn them apart.

Had Harris been infected when all that yellow gunk

oozed down onto him after he got trapped in the shed at Seth Harper's place? And if he *had* been infected, what did that mean? Was he becoming one of the monsters that Leo had been trying to warn them about? Was MECH-X4 going to have to fight Harris next?

No, that would be scientifically impossible, Harris thought.

Or would it?

Harris stared down at his arm, as captivated as he was concerned by its eerie glow. He didn't want to believe that he might actually be a threat to the MECH-X4 mission. And yet, after all he had already been through with Ryan, Spyder, and Mark . . . after all the doubts and shade he had thrown Ryan's way because his priorities hadn't seemed to be in the best interests of the whole team . . . it now seemed that *Harris* might end up being the one to break them apart. Or possibly even destroy them.